CU00842007

This book belongs to

....

First published in 2013 by Miles Kelly Publishing Ltd
Harding's Barn, Bardfield End Green, Thaxted, Essex, CM6 3PX, UK

Copyright © Miles Kelly Publishing Ltd 2013

2 4 6 8 10 9 7 5 3 1

Publishing Director Belinda Gallagher
Creative Director Jo Cowan
Editorial Director Rosie McGuire
Senior Designer Joe Jones
Production Manager Elizabeth Collins
Reprographics Stephan Davis, Jennifer Hunt, Thom Allaway

All rights reserved. No part of this publication may be reproduced, stored in a
retrieval system, or transmitted by any means, electronic, mechanical, photocopying,
recording or otherwise, without the prior permission of the copyright holder.

ISBN 978-1-78209-294-0

Printed in China

British Library Cataloguing-in-Publication Data
A catalogue record for this book is available from the British Library

ACKNOWLEDGEMENTS

The publishers would like to thank the following artists
who have contributed to this book:

Cover (main): Jacqueline East at The Bright Agency
Decorative banners (cover and throughout): asmjp from Shutterstock.com
Insides: Diana Mayo

Made with paper from a sustainable forest

www.mileskelly.net   info@mileskelly.net

www.factsforprojects.com

The Twelve Dancing Princesses

Miles
Kelly

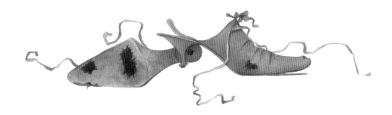

The king was puzzled. His twelve daughters were as beautiful as the moon and the stars, and he loved them all dearly. But every

morning they would appear
bleary-eyed and yawning,
with their shoes worn
through. Each night the king
would say good night and
lock the door behind him. So
how did they get out? And
where did they go?

Buying new shoes every day was costing a fortune, so the king issued a decree that said he would give the hand of one of his daughters in marriage to any man who could discover the secret. Failure to do so after three nights would mean banishment.

Plenty of young men were willing to risk being banished to win such a prize, but the princesses were too clever for

them. Before they went to bed, the princesses sang, and played musical instruments, and fed them sweetmeats and mead. And before the young men realized it, morning had come and there were the sleepy princesses and a large

pile of worn-out shoes.

The king was very cross.
Only the court shoemaker
remained cheerful.

One day a poor soldier
arrived in the kingdom. He
had heard of the decree and
wished to try his luck. As he

walked along the dusty road to the palace he met an old woman, and offered to share some of his food with her.

As they sat together the old woman asked where the soldier was bound. When he told her she said, "I may be

able to help you. Do not drink the mead the princesses offer you, for it is drugged. Pretend to be asleep, and you shall see what you shall see."

Then the old woman handed him a silvery cloak and said, "Whenever you wear this you will be invisible. Use it well!" With that she vanished, and the young man set off for the palace.

By now the king was tearing his hair out. The court shoemaker had taken on extra cobblers to keep up with the

demand for shoes, and the
princesses were still falling
asleep into their porridge
every morning.

The young man arrived and
was given dinner. He ate
heartily, but when the eldest
princess gave him mead he

only pretended to drink it.
Then he yawned loudly and
pretended to fall asleep.

Several footmen dumped
the soldier onto a bed placed
across the door of the
princesses' bedchamber. He
cautiously opened one eye

The Twelve Dancing Princesses

and gazed around the room.

The princesses were putting on beautiful dresses and jewels. They whispered to each other as they brushed their hair, powdered their noses and then pulled on the brand new shoes that had been delivered a few hours earlier.

Then the eldest princess clapped her hands three times. Instantly a trap door opened up in the floor and they all swiftly descended a steeply curving staircase. As soon as the last princess had

vanished the young man
flung on the cloak and rushed
after them.

   He found himself in a
beautiful garden where the
trees were covered in jewels,
sparkling in candlelight.
Musicians played whirling,

joyful tunes and all the princesses were dancing with the most charming and handsome princes.

The young man was spellbound, but he managed to keep his wits about him. He reached up and broke off a branch from one of the jewelled trees and hid it under his cloak. Then he ran back and lay down on his bed as though he had never stirred. So it happened again on the second night, and again on the third.

It was with a weary voice that the king asked the young man at breakfast on the fourth day if he had

found out where the
princesses went at night. But
the king sat up very quickly
when the young man told his
tale and produced the
branch from the jewelled tree.
   The king was delighted and
the young man chose the

youngest sister for his bride. And they all lived happily ever after. Except, of course, the court shoemaker, who always made the young man's shoes just a little too tight so they pinched.

The End